D0965094

SHOWSTOPPERS

SHOWSTOPPERS

An Emily Castles Mystery

HELEN SMITH

TYGER BOOKS

Copyright © Helen Smith 2011

This edition first published by Tyger Books in 2013

The right of Helen Smith to be identified as the author
of this work has been asserted by her in accordance with
the Copyright, Design and Patents Act 1988.

All rights reserved. No part of this publication may be
reproduced, stored in a retrieval system, or transmitted
in any form or by any means, electronic, mechanical,
photocopying, recording or otherwise, without the prior
permission of the copyright owner.

A CIP catalogue record for this book is available
from the British Library.

ISBN: 978-0956517067

For Lauren and Natasha

SHOWSTOPPERS

'Hello!' Emily called as she went into her flat on Friday evening, before the front door was fully closed behind her. She lived alone. Calling out was a deterrent strategy in case she had been followed home by an opportunistic thief. The thief was to assume, from hearing her cheery hello, that she lived with a tough, dangerous man or men who wouldn't stand for Emily being attacked on her doorstep or pushed inside and attacked there. It was a strategy that she no longer thought about or questioned, she just did it. It was one of many little survival tactics she had adopted since coming to live in London – but still, when she called out hello and got no answer, it always seemed, somehow, as if the silence was mocking her for living alone.

She picked up her mail from the doormat: a phone bill, a begging letter from a charity, a voucher for free delivery from a supermarket, and a letter addressed to her neighbour, Victoria. It wasn't unusual for Emily to get letters delivered to her that were meant for other residents of the street, as though the postmen at the local sorting office were conspiring to bring the community into closer contact with each other. She took the letter across the street to where Victoria lived in a three-storey red brick Edwardian terraced house with her husband and three sons. Emily Castles was a bright, clever young woman with a natural curiosity. When she walked anywhere she walked quickly, usually, and she looked up at her surroundings as if she expected to see something interesting at any minute. But today hadn't been a good day, and she looked down at the chewing gum-grey pavements without really seeing them, scuttling towards Victoria's house to avoid being seen as much as to avoid seeing anything. But Victoria opened the door to greet her before Emily could get away. Victoria was very slim, and she had naturally curly brown hair that fell to her shoulders in fat spirals. She was in her early-to-mid forties, Emily thought. Victoria rarely wore make-up unless it was a special occasion because she had lovely skin and even features, and she looked perfectly fine without it. She was bare-faced now, as usual, though Emily couldn't help noticing she looked paler than usual, even a little drawn.

'Letter for you,' said Emily.

'Oh God, no!' said Victoria. 'Oh my God!' She put one hand to the base of her throat and reached for the door behind her with the other, as if planning on whipping it off its hinges and using it as a shield. Her reaction was unexpected to say the least. 'Come in, Ems,' she said. 'Please.'

Emily longed to get back home so she could spend the evening on the sofa with a packet of ginger biscuits and a nice cup of tea, watching rubbish on TV.

'Please!'

Emily followed Victoria into the lovely kitchen, where the family ate most of their meals. Everything was just so, in a country-living kind of a way: there was a range oven *and* a conventional oven; cupboards and units painted in forget-me-not blue; French windows opening onto the garden at the back; big wooden storage boxes for the boys' Wellington boots and trainers; and something deliciously Italian-smelling (herbs and tomatoes and cheese in it or on it for sure, Emily thought) cooking in the oven.

Emily put the letter on the big scrubbed pine table. Victoria eyed it as though Emily had put a pet snake there. 'Will you open it for me?' Victoria said. 'Only I think it might be bad news.'

Victoria and Emily weren't close. Victoria was Emily's neighbour. Sometimes Emily looked in and fed the cat and watered the plants when the family was away. Sometimes she delivered letters to their house that had been delivered to her by mistake. If this letter contained bad news – a death in the family? An estrangement? Foreclosure? Bankruptcy? The expulsion of one of the boys from school? – then Emily was hardly the right person to open and read it and convey the news to Victoria. She took a seat and leaned her elbows on the table. She didn't pick up the letter.

'What about Piers? Can't he?'

'No!'

'But if it's bad news?'

'Not bad news so much as... danger.'

4

Victoria stood three feet away from the letter with her arms folded, staring at it nervously. She had a beautifully enunciated, ever-so-slightly-weary voice that suggested she had been bred to have servants and marry the kind of man who, in previous generations, might have joined the army and ordered his social inferiors to charge in vain against a better-armed enemy. Actually she had learned to speak that way in elocution lessons. Even so, even if she *had* belonged to some ruling class, surely she was anchored securely enough in modern times to understand that if she thought the letter contained anthrax, she shouldn't be so selfish as to propose that Emily open the letter on her behalf and take the hit?

Emily looked at the letter, but she didn't move. Danger? She couldn't think what Victoria could possibly mean. She hadn't had a good day, and in her tiredness and bewilderment she felt as though she were the stupid one.

'Not that kind of danger,' said Victoria, reading Emily's expression. She came and sat down at the table without unfolding her arms, hooking a chair and drawing it back with one foot, all of which was quite a difficult manoeuvre, a bit like Russian Cossack dancing. Only when she was sitting opposite Emily did Victoria unfold her arms, putting her elbows on the table and clasping her hands together in prayer before Emily. Then she confessed.

'I've been getting nasty notes. Poison pen. I can't bear to look at it. Can you?'

'Maybe Piers…?'

'Piers mustn't know. Quick, Ems, he'll be home from work soon. Please! Please. Open it for me. You're a clever girl. You'll know what to do.'

It wasn't a question, Emily thought, of whether or not she'd know what to do, but whether or not she wanted to get involved. Victoria didn't seem to think that was up for consideration. She seemed to think that Emily would want to spend her Friday night opening and screening Victoria's mail, spending her free time doing unwaged what she'd normally do during working hours to make a living.

She opened the letter.

The following message was printed in capital letters in blue biro on pale blue notepaper, the kind of stationery that you might use to write a thank you note if you were seventy years old:

WHAT A DISGRACE
TO THE RED, WHITE AND BLUE
VICTORIA'S BEEN NAUGHTY
WHAT SHALL WE DO?

There was no address or signature.

'It's another one, isn't it?' said Victoria, watching Emily's expression.

'I don't know. What were the other ones like?' She handed Victoria the letter so she could see for herself.

'I'll rip it up and put it on the compost heap – the slugs and snails can choke on it.'

'You can't do that. It's evidence. If you're being threatened, or blackmailed... Are you being blackmailed?'

'"Evidence?" I can't go to the police. What about Piers's job?'

Piers was something important, Emily wasn't quite sure what, in the civil service. 'Victoria, what does it mean?'

Victoria said, 'It seems to imply, doesn't it, with the "red, white and blue" that they'll cause a scandal and Piers's job with the government will be at stake.'

'Where are the other notes? If someone's threatening you, you can't let them get away with it.'

Victoria brought her large, grey handbag over from where it had been squatting on the Welsh dresser, in front of the slightly dusty display of never-used blue-and-white crockery. She said, 'You know I used to be an actress?'

Yes. Everyone knew it. Victoria still had the cheekbones. She had done a bit of telly when she was younger, and popped up now and then in daytime repeats, in *Rumpole of the Bailey* or other dependable, once-popular British TV series. For whatever reason – love, Emily had always assumed – she had given it up, but now she ran a stage school locally, so the subject quite often came up, and even if people didn't watch much daytime TV, every one of her neighbours knew what she had once been.

'I made a video,' said Victoria. 'When I was a student...' She curled her fingers and put her hand up to her mouth and looked out of the window, her knuckles pressed against her lips as if to silence herself. Then she put her arms around herself and hugged tightly. Emily was impressed and slightly thrilled to be treated to this private performance of Victoria playing 'woman for whom the memory of a youthful transgression is still painful'. She tried to think of a tactful way to say that no one would much care these days if a video of Victoria's bare bottom should show up on the Internet, unless she was really famous. The world was awash with pornography – Victoria's indiscretions would matter to no one but her.

'If it got onto the Internet,' said Victoria, 'I would be ruined.'

'It may not be as bad as you think,' said Emily. 'People these days are very broad-minded.'

'I'd say they're less broad-minded than they were twenty years ago. But that's hardly the point. Emily, a man died because of that video.' She stood, turned and did a press-lipped anguished face, and wrung her hands together. By now, all Emily's earlier cares had seeped away because she was so thoroughly absorbed by Victoria's elegant response to her troubles. Solo performances by actors of Victoria's calibre would do brilliantly well as part of executive redundancy packages, Emily reflected. If she were more entrepreneurial, she'd be off and making some phone calls about it now, setting up a new business. Instead, she said, 'A man died? Is that why you gave up acting?'

'God, no! The cost of child care in this country...'

'Besides, you've got Showstoppers now.'

'Not for much longer if these notes continue.' Victoria brought out two more notes from an inner pocket in her handbag and showed them to Emily. Like the one she had just opened, these contained sneering rhymes written on blue stationery.

> I KNOW VICTORIA'S SECRET
> I HOPE I CAN KEEP IT
> IF I SHOULD LEAK IT
> SHE WILL BE SORRY

And

> WHEN THEY KNOW WHAT I KNOW
> IT WILL STOP THE SHOW
> AT SHOWSTOPPERS

'Not exactly W H Auden, is it?' said Victoria. 'I can't show them to Piers. He did English at Oxford. He'd be mortified.'

'Has the sender made any demands for money?'

'Not yet.'

'It could be a bluff. Who else knows about the video?'

'I haven't told a living soul about it, Emily. The only people who knew about it were my boyfriend and me because we were in it. We filmed it ourselves. We didn't even hire a lighting guy.'

Emily was quiet for a while, thinking about what sort of person even considers hiring a lighting technician when filming *that* sort of video. Victoria watched her respectfully in her turn, as if Emily were mentally sifting through the evidence and would soon have a solution.

'Why would anyone send you something like that, Victoria?'

'I don't know *why*, but I know *who*. It's my old boyfriend, David. It has to be. I haven't seen him in twenty years or more, suddenly he turns up at the school. Next thing, I'm getting nasty notes through the mail.'

'He turned up at the school? What did he say?'

'I didn't talk to him. I just saw his name on the enrolment forms – he wants to get his daughter into Showstoppers. Or so he claims. I don't know if he even has a daughter.'

'You think he's stalking you? What does he want?'

'That's what we've got to find out.'

We? Emily had only popped across the road to deliver a letter. Suddenly she was being roped into investigating Victoria's possibly sordid relations with a possibly dangerous ex-boyfriend. And come to think of it, Victoria herself was possibly dangerous, too.

'You said someone had died?' said Emily.

But they were interrupted by the sound of the key in the lock, the front door opening, and then a hearty 'Hello!' in Piers's voice. Victoria half-rose from her chair and tucked the letters and envelopes into the back pocket of her jeans. As she sank back down again, she gave Emily a warning look.

'I think you should tell him,' whispered Emily. 'A secret's only really useful currency to a blackmailer when it remains a secret. Could there have been a mistake about the man who died? Maybe you're not responsible.'

'Oh yes! I hope so. That would be a weight off my mind after twenty years. But who do I ask? I can hardly go to the police.'

'Was it an accident? A car crash, something like that?'

Victoria listened for sounds of her husband outside, her head to one side, her finger on her lips. They heard Piers's footsteps in the corridor as he went about his normal just-back-home routine: hanging up his coat, finding a place for his laptop computer, washing his hands in the sink in the downstairs bathroom. In the long pause before she spoke, Emily thought again of Victoria's training as an actress – it was a very suspenseful pause. 'No,' said Victoria. 'He died laughing.'

Victoria was such a humourless person that Emily was impressed. She longed to know more, but there was no chance of it now.

'Hello, Emily,' said Piers, coming into the kitchen. 'Had a good week?'

'My contract came to an end today.'

'Oh, Emily,' said Victoria. 'I'm sorry. I didn't know. What a shame.'

'Bad luck!' said Piers.

'Oh, it's OK. It was only temporary anyway. Back to the agency on Monday.'

'Could you do some work at the school? Victoria always needs a hand there.'

'Yes!' said Victoria. 'Please do.'

'That's nice of you,' said Emily. 'But I need something long-term.'

'Oh, please! You'd be doing me a favour. I'm going to need help interviewing the new parents.' Victoria gave a 'special' look to Emily, but she needn't have bothered. Emily knew very well why Victoria wanted her at the school. Instead of getting a nice job at a proper office with a canteen, she was supposed to go and help out at Victoria's stage school and learn more, if that were possible, about her neighbour's life than she already knew – which was considerably more than she wanted to know.

Piers went to the fridge and opened a bottle of white wine. He got out three glasses, which was a good start. If you were thirsty, you could die from the want of a cup of tea or a glass of wine when

Victoria was hosting. 'It would set my mind at rest to have a friend of Victoria's working there,' he said.

Emily wasn't friends with Victoria. Victoria sometimes gave her hand-me-down, very expensive, brightly-coloured twinsets. But friends? No.

'She gets very stressed when she's planning the end-of-term "extravaganza",' said Piers. 'Always threatens to close the school or flounce off and let someone else run it.' He filled a glass with wine and handed it to Victoria. 'I wish you would give it up, Vee. There are so many other things you could be doing if you didn't have the school – things we could be doing together.'

'I don't know why I do it: parents, patrons, prize-giving, tap-dancing, teenagers, toddlers, teachers' skits. *Stress*. And that's just the showcase. I'm also battling the landlord because he wants to sell up. The bills are sky-high. The infant toilets keep blocking up, and there's something wrong with the electrics that needs to be fixed by nine o'clock tomorrow morning. I'm *this close* to giving the place up and letting someone else run it. And now there's this other thing.'

'What other thing?' Piers asked.

'I could take you in and introduce you tomorrow,' said Victoria to Emily. 'We do weekends and after-school and school holidays, but tomorrow is our end-of-term showcase for the students at Showstoppers – it's a chance for them to put together everything they've learned – and we use it to recruit new students, too. Oh... I'll be OK when it's over and we go off on holiday. I love it, really. You'll love it, too. And the kids will love you. Do you dance?'

Emily said, 'No.'

'What other thing?' said Piers again.

Victoria looked at Emily, then she stood and took the poison pen letters from her back pocket and spread them out on the table.

'Crumbs!' said Piers. 'Not much of a poet, is she? Or he. Who's sending these, do you think?' He went and put his arm around Victoria's waist, glass of wine held at chin height in his other hand, and they stood together and looked at the notes as though they were at the private view of an art exhibition, trying to make sense of a perplexing exhibit.

'You remember I told you about David Devereux, my old boyfriend? We made a video together when we were students.'

'Did you?' Piers blushed, the pink patches on his cheeks girlishly endearing, as if he had put on a pair of pink fluffy slippers. 'I've never seen it.' He broke away from Victoria and sat down and drank a mouthful of his wine.

'Not that kind of video,' said Victoria. 'It was a performance piece for our degree. We began to wish we'd never made it. It brought everyone who watched it the most awful bad luck.' Victoria looked over towards the Welsh dresser. 'I don't even like to touch it, to be honest.'

'It's here?' said Piers. He went over to the dresser. It was obviously a dumping-ground for all sorts of once-useful or might-one-day-be-useful items. Piers crouched and opened the double doors at the bottom of the dresser and brought out: a ball of string, a cricket ball, an electric screwdriver – 'Oh! I've been looking for that!' – a roll of cellotape, a packet of plastic clothes pegs, four electric light bulbs... 'No,' he said, shovelling it all back in again. 'Can't see a video.'

'In the top drawer. With the pizza leaflets.' Victoria watched while Piers rummaged for a bit and then pulled an old VHS tape out of the drawer and brought it over to the table. She said, 'It was twenty years ago. I'd almost forgotten about it, but then it arrived in the post a week or so ago. The widow of my old tutor sent it to me. She's getting on a bit, and she's got to move into a care home. She found it when she was clearing out her house. There was a lovely note with it, saying, "I don't blame you for what happened to Bill."'

'Is the note anything like these ones?' asked Emily.

'No, unfortunately. Or fortunately. She was a really nice woman.'

'Why is it bad luck?' Piers asked.

'Well, David and I always believed that Bill – my old tutor – died because of it. And then we split up – though that's a good thing, in hindsight. Or I'd never have met you. It just seemed like one thing after another. Though death is much worse, of course, than the breakup of a love affair between two drama students.'

'He died because of your video?' said Piers. 'What on earth do you mean, Vee?'

'He had to evaluate it for our degree. It really was the most awful, earnest piece of tosh. An interpretive dance piece – we were very proud of it, of course, at the time. But we showed it to a few of the other students, and they cracked up laughing at it. My friend Gloria had an asthma attack – they had to take her to the walk-in health clinic and put her on the nebulizer. Then poor old Bill had a heart attack and died while he was watching it. They found him sitting in his arm chair in front of the TV, with this awful rictus grin.'

'Surely they didn't mention the awful rictus grin in the coroner's report?' said Piers.

'No. But that's what we heard afterwards from his wife – his widow. Everyone teased us, all the other students. They said he died laughing. I don't doubt it's true. Honestly, I can't bear to have it in the house. And now this business with the poison pen letters. What shall I do with the ghastly thing?'

'There's no such thing as bad luck brought by a video. Your tutor would have died anyway, Victoria, if he had a weak heart. You know that. You know what we ought to do? We'll watch it now – prove there's nothing in it.'

'Is it very long?' asked Emily. 'The video?'

'It's VHS,' said Victoria. 'We haven't got a machine that will play it in the house.'

'Have *you*, Emily?' asked Piers. He seemed ready for action.

Fortunately Emily only had a DVD player. But it seemed a good time to take her leave. 'I have some errands to run in the morning,' she said, meaning that she would like to stay in bed. 'But I could be at Showstoppers by ten o'clock tomorrow to help out.'

'That would be great!' said Victoria. Emily relaxed a bit – actually it might be quite nice to work for Victoria for a while. She smiled. The fragrant, delicious, very cold, expensive white wine that Piers had dispensed for her in a heavy, expensive wine glass had worked its magic on her. But then Victoria delivered her punch line, 'Unfortunately the children will start coming in around ten o'clock. It's best if I introduce you to the staff before that. Shall we say eight thirty-ish?'

The next morning, as she was on her way to Showstoppers shortly before ten o'clock (with Piers's help, she'd managed to talk Victoria into letting her have a later start), Emily saw her neighbour Dr. Muriel on the other side of the street. 'Lovely day for a wedding!' called Dr. Muriel, waving her stick in the air when she saw Emily. Dr.

Muriel was a middle-aged feminist who lived alone. She was wearing a tweed skirt with a grass stain just above the hem, where she had knelt to weed her herbaceous border after cutting the lawn, going down on her right knee to do it like an old-fashioned suitor. Emily took a few moments to try to evaluate Dr. Muriel's comment. Given her appearance and her independent nature, Emily thought it unlikely that Dr. Muriel was on her way to a take part in a ceremony that would seal her future to that of a man or woman. Emily herself wasn't getting married. But it was a sunny day, and it was a Saturday, and someone, somewhere would be getting wed. Therefore she deduced that Dr. Muriel was just making a slightly obtuse remark that didn't merit a reply. This was not unusual. Emily waved back as if to say, 'Noted!' and she did it with a smile on her face in case it was a joke, to show that she had got it and she was amused. Dr. Muriel was one of those people who could help to simplify an idea and provide an answer to a problem if one were needed – and if not, she could complicate everything needlessly. Emily wasn't in the mood for complications or cryptic remarks. She went on her way.

But Dr. Muriel swooped across the road – a big, grey owl, Emily her helpless quarry. Why was everyone so friendly? You didn't move to London to have a chat. You moved to London to get on in life and get invited to sophisticated parties – not that Emily had had much success with either, to date.

'Terrible business!' said Dr. Muriel to Emily.

'Yes,' said Emily, not quite sure what she was talking about.

'You're a bright girl. You'll find something that's right for you...' Dr. Muriel saw that Emily had abandoned any attempt to pretend she understood the topic of conversation. She said, 'Vicky told me you were out of work again.'

Emily said, 'You should see the job adverts these days – it's all about "passion" and "commitment" and "making a difference". I'd just like to find an employer that will pay me a decent wage for doing a competent job. I don't want to give up a piece of my soul.'

'You rail against potential employers who treat their trivial business as though it were important, and yet you treat your important business – your life, your future – as though it were trivial. You most certainly do not just want to do "a competent job", Emily Castles. You are an inquisitive, fair-minded, insightful young woman who is easily bored. It's true that employers are continually letting you go, but it's because you have let them go long before it ever comes to that. You could do worse than go and work for Vicky, m'dear. There are always interesting dynamics in a staffroom (I should know), and of course, there are all those pushy parents intent on polishing pebbles and producing diamonds in two lessons a week during term-times, for £20 a week. I think you'll find it stimulating. I hope so, anyway.'

Emily would have liked to confide in Dr. Muriel about the blackmail and Victoria's video. But she had only known this secret for less than a day, and she didn't think it would be to her credit to spill it to the very next person she saw after Victoria told her about it. Instead she said, 'So are you going to a wedding?'

'Gracious, no! Weddings are awfully depressing, aren't they? They do have a tendency to make one feel suicidal. No, indeed. This afternoon I shall be attending an event that always makes me feel positively murderous.' And Dr. Muriel smiled wickedly and went on her way.

Showstoppers was in a red and yellow brick Edwardian building not far from the street where Emily lived. It would be pleasant to walk to work, she acknowledged – and it would be strange to be walking to school after all these years, even if it was to a performing arts school. Emily enjoyed a pleasant little frisson of nostalgia as she thought back to the days when she walked to school as a child in her blazer and grey and blue school uniform. It had always seemed sunny. For a moment she wondered whether this was a kind of false memory – the rosiness of an adult reflecting on her childhood – and then she realised that she probably only remembered sunny days walking to school because she would have got a lift when it was raining.

Victoria came out to greet her when she arrived at Showstoppers, gripping Emily by the shoulders and giving her a kiss on one cheek. She was wearing jeans and a white T-shirt, with a hideous pewter-grey loose-knit shawl draped over her shoulders that made her look fragile and tragic, as though her husband had been lost at sea and she had grabbed just *anything* to wear to keep herself warm while she walked along the shoreline, waiting for news of him. 'Hello, Ems,' said Victoria. 'Listen, you won't tell anyone here that I killed a man?'

'No,' said Emily. 'I won't do that.'

The dance school had once been a local primary school, so it had several large, airy rooms with wooden floors and high ceilings, a performance space where assemblies had been held, and a suite of tiny toilets for small children, as well as standard-sized facilities. The offices were upstairs on the first floor. It had been a long time since Emily had been in a place like this. She had forgotten about the shiny thick linoleum on the stairs, the worn banisters, the scratched wooden floors in the classrooms. From downstairs there drifted the plangent sound of the piano being played by unknown hands, and over the music she heard the excited, almost-mocking sound of children's laughter, and she was struck again with memories, as though the school was full of ghosts whispering about P.E. lessons and colouring-in.

Victoria opened the door to the office. 'Let me introduce you girls to each other,' she said in her weary, posh voice. 'People say "girls" now, right? I've been "a woman" since I was eighteen, but that was in the eighties. I've lived so long, we've all become girls again. I would say it's like a fabulous rejuvenation cream – except it only recategorizes you, it doesn't remove your wrinkles.'

Emily smiled at the girl behind the desk and raised her eyebrows to signal that she was slightly baffled. Did Victoria always go on like this?

'I'm Seema,' said the girl behind the desk, ignoring Emily's eyebrows. The trousers Seema were wearing were as white as her teeth, and her smile was as big as her hair, which had been backcombed and sprayed until it stood an inch above her scalp. She was plump and pretty. 'I don't mind being called a girl. They can chuck me in my grave when I'm ninety and say "here lies the old girl" and I won't mind. But then I won't mind about anythink much, will I, if I'm dead? You feeling old today, Victoria?'

'I am a bit.'

'Thought so. You only mention the nineteen eighties when you're feeling old. Ready for your holiday after this? You can have a nice rest.'

'Emily's here to help out while I'm away.'

'Yeah? Me and Emily'll run the place smooth as ice cream and twice as sweet, Victoria.'

'You are a darling, Seema. What would I do without you? It's too, too stressful.'

'About time you got some fresh air on them frown lines. Forget about this place next week, it's in capable hands. You'll come back and you'll wonder why you don't leave everythink to us every day.'

Seema was a white-trousered steamroller, trundling over all of Victoria's anxieties – and some of her self-esteem – and crushing them all, cheerfully.

Victoria picked up a folder from Seema's desk. She held it as far away from her face as she could to read it.

'You want your glasses on, Victoria,' said Seema.

'Oh, I know. I'm too vain. I think I'd rather be fitted with extendable arms than wear my reading glasses. Is this the list of new clients? I'd like Emily to interview the parents, get a feel for how we do things.'

'You want Emily to do the induction? What's she gonna say if she don't know the place?'

'Not an induction exactly... asking questions: a screening process.'

'*They're* supposed to ask questions, and *we're* supposed to have the answers. That's how it works usually, innit?'

'Oh, Seema. You are so terribly efficient,' said Victoria. 'But I think we should introduce a screening process, don't you? Whittle out the undesirables.'

'Undie-what? That's not a word your accountant would understand, Victoria. The bills don't pay themselves.'

'Actually, I rather think they do, with these electronic systems and direct debit and whatnot.'

'So long as they pay termly in advance, they're desirable, ent they?' Seema took the folder from Victoria and read aloud from it. 'Dolly, Kayleigh, Maqsood, Robin, DeShawn. Four, five, six years old, these kids – what harm can they do?'

'It's not the children I wanted to screen, so much as the parents...'

'I don't want Emily turning away potential clients because she's unfamiliar with how to run an establishment like this. No offence, Emily.'

How many jobs had Emily started where she had soon enough discovered that there was some kind of polite feud going on, with undercurrents of tension about who was really in charge and how things should be run? Too many; most of them; all of them. The thing about being here – or anywhere – on a temporary contract was that, ultimately, *she didn't care*. She smiled at Seema: a genuine, warm smile. Seema was posturing. Emily wanted to let her know that she, Emily, wasn't a threat.

'No, of course,' Victoria said, more vague than contrite. She picked up her handbag and felt around in it before bringing out something that Emily recognised: the video. 'Can you put this somewhere safe for me? Lock it away?' Victoria said to Seema.

'Is it for the show?' Seema said. 'I'll have to get Dizzy to bring the video cart down. I don't know if we've even got the screen set up.'

'Crikey, no! It's just something that needs to be locked away, very carefully, out of sight. I don't want it in the house. I can't deal with it now. I'll worry about it when I get back from holiday.'

'Oh?' said Seema. She looked as though she were about to burst out of her trousers with curiosity.

'Dirty video, is it? Found Piers's porn stash?' The dreadlocked head of a smiling man who Emily hadn't even noticed emerged with regal sedateness from behind Seema's desk, where he had been working on a cluster of electrical plug sockets set into the floor in the office. He was in his forties, tiny strands of silver hair twisted in among the black, as though his locks were magnetic and had attracted a powdering of iron filings that had been spilled on the floor near where he had knelt to work. He held a screwdriver and wore very dark blue overalls that had a few daubs of paint on them. There was no doubt in Emily's mind that he was the school's handyman. In fact, he did a bit of everything – technician, electrician, carpenter, caretaker and occasional chauffeur. He was indispensable because of his willingness to turn his hand to anything, though he wasn't especially skilled at any of them.

'Nothing like that, Dizzy,' Victoria said. 'It's a video I made when I was a student, with my boyfriend at the time, David Devereux. I don't want anyone to see it.'

'Oh!' said Seema.

Dizzy said respectfully, 'An acting video? My mistake, Victoria. Hello, Emily.'

Victoria said, 'Dizzy, you're not trying to fix the electrics yourself, are you? You need someone qualified.'

'Mr. Barrymore's helping me,' said Dizzy.

'Barry's helping you?' Victoria put her hands palm-out in front of her and made a 'window-washing' movement, fingers spread wide, as if trying to wipe away Dizzy's words where they hung in the air between them both. 'You *are* joking? Please don't let him anywhere near it. He's more likely to sabotage it than fix it. You know he wants me out of this place. I noticed the infant toilets didn't get blocked up once when he was away for his fortnight in Menorca.' She turned to Emily and said, 'Mr. Barrymore, our *horrible* landlord, is trying to get me to give this place up so he can sell it to developers to be made into luxury flats.'

Emily said, 'Hello, Dizzy.'

Seema said, 'I'm studying for a City & Guilds in building maintenance. I'd take a look at the wiring myself but I'm too busy.'

'Of course you are,' Victoria said. 'Right! I need to go and get changed. I need to rehearse the teachers' skit with Graham, he's over-creaking his Tin Man in my *Wizard of Oz* tap-dancing routine. He doesn't even have to tap dance, just gyrate his hips a bit. Some of the children have already arrived, and the rest will be arriving any minute. We've got the patrons coming in to give prizes. They'll need to be briefed. We've got the new parents coming; they'll need to be interviewed. We've got the current parents coming; they'll need to be avoided, especially if their children aren't being awarded prizes.'

There was suddenly a very unpleasant smell in the room. 'Oh my goodness!' said Victoria. 'What's that? Don't tell me we've got a problem with the drains?'

A sweaty white man with a bald head edged into the room – apparently he had been standing in the doorway for a short while. The man was about fifty years old, and he was wearing an England football shirt, which was made of white synthetic material with three blue lions embroidered on the left breast. Emily didn't recognise him and, given his age and physical condition, was inclined to disbelieve he played for the team. She took a dislike to him: she didn't approve of snoops. 'I think it's Precious,' the man said. 'I've been feeding her extra sausages to get her to be good.'

'Barry,' Victoria said, 'what on *earth* is Precious doing here?'

'You said you needed a real dog to play Toto,' Seema said. 'Mr. Barrymore's was the only one available at short notice. It seemed the best thing to do.'

'No trouble at all,' said Mr. Barrymore. 'Specially as we're only next door.'

Victoria walked around the desk behind Seema, and Emily followed her to see an extraordinarily ugly bulldog lying on a blanket. The dog sighed.

'If you brought this malodorous animal onto the premises as your first step in an eviction plan, you're more cunning than I thought,' said Victoria, opening a window in the office.

Mr. Barrymore laughed appreciatively and for slightly too long, as though he had met his favourite TV comedienne by chance in the supermarket and she had said something funny about the vegetables in his shopping basket. He said, 'There's another place I want you to look at in Crystal Palace, Victoria. Very modern. Much better appointed than this. I don't need Precious to persuade you. Soon as you see it, you'll love it.'

Victoria said, 'I'm going to get changed. Emily, do you know Morgana Blakely, the romance novelist?'

'I've heard of her,' said Emily. 'Is she coming?'

'Yes. She's Piers' aunty, and she'll be giving a prize to one of the students. You'll know her when you see her. She'll be wearing something ridiculous. Probably a hat.' From downstairs there was the sound of someone on the piano playing "Somewhere Over the Rainbow". Victoria listened for a moment and then continued, 'You know Dr. Muriel? And Midori? Midori's a Japanese girl. Goes by the stage name of DJ Hana-bi?'

'Yes,' said Emily. 'They both live on our street. I didn't know they were friends of yours.'

'Friends and neighbours and awfully good role models. They'll be giving prizes, too. They'll be along in a bit, so can you just keep them out of mischief? I can hear Samuel giving us a very big hint on the piano. I need to find Graham and get started rehearsing. Seema, dear, you can take care of the parents, but *please* will you let Emily talk to David Devereux when he gets here.'

'David Devereux's coming? Fella was in that spy thing? Black geezer? I thought he was in Hollywood.' Mr. Barrymore seemed impressed.

'Yes. So if you would be a love and get the electrics working? I don't know what's wrong with the wiring. I don't want the music cutting out when the tinies are doing their Flight of the Bumblebee. Graham and I can improvise, but the little ones can't – nor can the teenagers, come to that – and I don't want them being upset.'

Seema said, 'I need to talk to you, Victoria. There's a letter arrived here for you. It's a bit of a strange one. It's a personal letter, but I didn't realise. I'm afraid I opened it.'

'Oh, not now, Seema,' Victoria said. 'I really can't be doing with it.'

Victoria left. Mr. Barrymore left. Dizzy left. Seema said, 'Emily, have you seen that video? I need to lock it away somewhere. It was here on the desk.'

From downstairs came the sound of Victoria shouting, "Emileeeeeeee, Emileeeeeee. Can you come down? Morgana's here.'

Emily said to Seema, 'It can't have gone far. Can it?'

When Emily went downstairs to meet the famous romance novelist, Morgana Blakely, she immediately recognised her, just as Victoria had said she would. Morgana was indeed wearing a hat. It was a miniature top hat perched on the side of her head and held in place with hat pins and with a short veil attached to it, fashioned out of wire mesh. Emily had been to parties (or rather, she had waitressed at them) where canapés were served in the form of miniature fish and chips, or miniature burgers roughly the size of the circle made by joining the thumb and forefinger of one hand. Morgana's top hat was a bit like this. It had all the attributes of a normal top hat, but it was considerably smaller. If Morgana wasn't so imposing and hadn't just arrived to give prizes at her nephew's wife's stage school, Emily would have assumed she was in fancy dress.

Morgana must have been in her sixties – at least – but she had the youthful-looking skin of a woman who moisturises every day. She wore a purple trouser suit with a long purple velvet coat over it, trimmed in mauve marabou stork feathers, and she had applied flattering make-up: pale pink lipstick, black mascara, a touch of mauve eye shadow and a dusting of pink blusher. Her short, stylish hair was the colour of rich beef gravy.

Before Emily had to worry what to do with her, Dr. Muriel arrived. She and Morgana greeted each other like old friends, which is to say, they held hands, looked into each other's eyes and laughed.

Victoria came up to them. She was now wearing a blue pinafore dress and sparkly red tap shoes. She had put her hair in two long plaits, and she was still working at the strands of the left one as she walked.

'Something terrible has happened,' she said. 'I think we should call the whole thing off.'

'You always say that,' said Morgana. 'Things come together in the end, don't they?'

'No, it's worse than under-rehearsed dancers and disgruntled parents. I think we might be in danger. There's this video I made when I was a student...'

'Oh, Victoria!' said Morgana.

'Not that kind of video.'

'Who knows about it?' asked Dr. Muriel.

'I haven't told anyone,' Victoria said. 'Not a living soul.'

Emily checked her pulse. Yes, still alive.

Victoria said, 'It was a video I made with David Devereux when we were at drama school. He's been sending me poison pen letters.'

'Has he, indeed?' said Dr. Muriel.

'Bad things happen to people who watch that video.'

'How interesting,' said Dr. Muriel. 'Have you ever heard of a self-fulfilling prophesy?'

Morgana said, 'Tell us what happened, Victoria, in the order it happened.'

'I made the video with David. Twenty years ago a man died of a heart attack from laughing so much while he was watching it. David and I broke up even though we loved each other. The video turned up at the house a few weeks ago. David tried to enrol his daughter in the school a few weeks later. And then I started getting the letters.'

'You think David's still in love with you? He's invented a daughter and come back to claim you, and sending those letters is his way of doing it?' Morgana asked.

'We don't know for sure that David Devereux sent those letters,' said Emily.

A man whose face had been covered in silver face paint came up to Victoria. His limbs were encased in silver-sprayed cardboard, and he was wearing a small silver triangular hat. His costume was a boiler suit and a pair of Wellington boots. These had also been sprayed with silver paint. He said to Victoria, 'Midori just phoned. She's ill. She can't make it.'

'You see?' wailed Victoria. 'More bad luck!'

'I don't think it's anything to do with the video,' said the Tin Man. 'She's at home. She can't have seen it. Tummy trouble, she said.' And then, to Emily, 'Hello. I'm Graham.'

'Graham knows about the video?' asked Emily.

'Yes,' said Victoria. 'I had to tell him I'd brought it into the school. I think if you don't tell employees about this sort of thing – potential hazards in the workplace – you can get in trouble. Health and Safety.'

'I doubt the video *is* dangerous, Victoria,' said Dr. Muriel. 'Would it help dispel the myth if we were to watch it?'

'The video has disappeared,' said Victoria. 'It's out in the wild, so to speak, and now anyone could just pick it up and watch it, unawares.'

'Anyone with a VHS video player,' said Emily.

'Precious has disappeared,' Victoria continued. 'Dizzy has disappeared. Mr. Barrymore is still here. I wish he would disappear – I'd make him disappear myself if I could, though not until after he has fixed my electrics. As for Dizzy, he's what you might call a "bodger", but he does get things done in the end, and I do need to find him.'

'Seema said she might be able to fix the wiring,' said Emily. 'Shall I find her and ask her to do it?'

'I wish I could leave everything to Seema. Isn't she marvellous? But she's doing the induction with the parents. Emily, do you think you could have a look for Precious? You like dogs – can you see if you can coax her out? She's an evil-looking bulldog with a very low undercarriage. She stinks. Her name's Precious. Have you got a sausage or something to tempt her with when you find her?'

Emily did not. She thought she might not go and look for Precious. She said, 'I already met the dog, remember?'

'Oh, yes. I'm so stressed. I'm getting confused about things. Thank goodness you're here, Ems.'

Morgana said, 'What a shame I don't write mysteries, I could be noting all this down. It only really gets interesting for me when the love interest crops up. Can you do anything about that, Victoria?'

Just then, as if waiting for his cue – he was an actor, after all – the most handsome man Emily had ever seen walked through the door, accompanied by a small, beautiful, caramel-coloured child. It was David Devereux and Dolly. Dolly had long, curly hair that sprang out from her head as though someone had opened it to try to understand the workings and hadn't been able to fit everything back in again. David had eyes, hands, lips, teeth, a smile, a chest, a waist, long legs and strong arms – just like any other man, really. But the way they had all been put together seemed so much more appealing.

'Oh, Muriel,' said Morgana Blakely. 'Here's your answer, if you ever ask yourself why we agree to do these things – you've got your self-fulfilling prophesy video conundrum. And I've got this.'

'Hello, Victoria,' said David. They greeted each other like former lovers who still cared about each other, which is to say, they held hands and looked into each other's eyes, strange, tender expressions on their faces, as though they weren't sure whether they ought to say sorry about something.

'Emily,' Victoria said eventually, 'this is David. Would you mind looking after him? And Dolly, do you want to come with me and find some of the other children? One of the teachers will show you around. You can see how you like the place.'

'Victoria!' called David before she had gone too far. 'Did you ever have children?'

Victoria turned, Dolly's hand in hers. 'Yes,' she said. 'Three sons.'

She turned, and they walked away. Sunlight streamed from the tall windows along the corridor and dripped coppery highlights into Victoria's plaits and Dolly's liquorice-coloured curly hair: a woman dressed as a child from a story about a tornado-induced dream holding onto the hand of a child who was so beautiful Emily thought she looked as though she'd be able to create tornadoes and stories of her own one day.

'Emily!' whispered Dr. Muriel, interrupting Emily's reverie. 'I wanted to ask you about these letters Victoria's been receiving. We can't do it now. Shall we try to find a moment?'

'Seema could probably show you one,' Emily said. 'They've been coming to Victoria's house, but apparently one arrived at the school this morning.'

'Indeed? That's most interesting.' She turned to Morgana and indicated that they should head upstairs to the office. 'Shall we?'

'Must we?' said Morgana. She gave a little wave to Emily and David, and she took Dr. Muriel's arm as they walked up the stairs.

'Nice place,' said David to Emily. 'How long have you been working here?'

'About an hour.'

David laughed as though it was the cleverest thing anyone had ever said to him. Somewhere in the background, as more and more students arrived to take part in the show, Emily heard the sound of children's joyful voices, as though they had heard David laughing and wanted to join in. Emily was surrounded by an orchestra of happy sounds. It was all a bit disconcerting, but there was one thing she was sure of: it wasn't David who had sent those poison pen letters.

'Can I do anything useful?' asked David. It seemed a rhetorical question – what couldn't he do, with that smile? But Emily rallied and said, 'A dog's gone missing. You could help me find her.'

'I don't know much about dogs.'

Emily thought of her dog Jessie, her lovely old Golden Retriever who had died. She still missed Jessie and had thought her heart would break when she watched Jessie slip away, enfeebled by illness at the end. She said, 'Sometimes I think I know too much.'

'Come on, then! We'll make a great team. You don't mind if I keep my mobile on? I'm expecting a call from LA. They're probably not up and about this time of the morning. But you never know: the city that never sleeps.'

'Isn't that New York?'

David laughed again. 'There you go. Another thing you know more about than I do. We'll make a great team.'

Seema came bustling by, white trousers gleaming, floral top flowing. She was carrying a packet of dog biscuits and Dizzy's screwdriver. 'David!' she said. 'What an honour to meet you. I loved your work in *Spies Like Us*'. She smiled. She looked vivacious. Emily felt unaccountably jealous. Seema said, 'Emily, do you want a Bonio?'

Emily said, 'I'm trying to give them up.'

David laughed (again) and took the packet of dog biscuits. 'Good thinking. Seema, is it? Did I talk to you on the phone about enrolling Dolly? Don't worry, we'll find your dog.'

'It isn't my dog!' said Seema, horrified, as though he'd said 'Don't worry, we'll find your Nazi memorabilia.' Emily didn't much trust people who didn't like dogs. People who didn't know much about dogs were OK, of course. But there's nothing admirable about someone who tips over into active dislike. 'Our handyman's gone missing,' Seema continued. 'Black dude, blue overalls, dreads. If you see him...?'

David put his hand, almost, on Emily's waist as he escorted her out of the room. 'Don't worry,' he said to Seema. 'If we see him, we'll send him your way.'

'I'm doing the induction for the new parents,' Seema said. 'Most of them are here now. I do hope you'll join us, David.'

'Yeah, I will. Not sure if this place is quite right for Dolly, yet.'

Seema gasped in anguish and put one hand to her face as though he had slapped her.

'Kidding!' he said. 'I'm kidding, Seema. It's a great place. Any questions, though, I might as well ask Emily.'

Seema gave Emily a look of general disdain – so it was impossible to know whether she disapproved of Emily spending time with David or whether she simply felt that Emily couldn't be trusted to answer any questions about the school correctly (in which assessment she was, after all, perfectly correct). Then she bustled off again.

'I need to talk to Dr. Muriel before we go looking for Precious,' Emily said to David, leading the way up the stairs to the office. 'She and Morgana have been looking at a weird letter that arrived here for Victoria this morning.'

David didn't react – at least, he didn't react the way someone would react if they were responsible for sending the letter. He said, 'Is there anything about this place that isn't a little bit weird?'

When they got to the office, they saw that Dr. Muriel and Morgana had made themselves comfortable. They were drinking tea and chatting earnestly. There was a very large oval dish of sandwiches on the desk beside them, its cling film cover partially pulled back and several of the sandwiches missing.

'Where is Seema?' asked Dr. Muriel. 'The sandwich shop just delivered these. I think we need to fend for ourselves rather than get faint with hunger. Emily, you've been here all day, haven't you? I know it's barely midday, but if you don't eat now, it will be four o'clock before the show's over.

You'll be hungry if you don't eat a couple of sandwiches now.'

'I think we need to do something to help Victoria,' Dr. Muriel said. 'Poor woman is in meltdown.'

'I wish Piers were here,' said Morgana. 'But he's so often working on weekends.'

'Is Piers her husband?' asked David. 'Matinees are a killer. Is he in a show in town?'

'He's not an actor. I'm not quite sure what he does exactly. He's in the civil service.'

'Is he?' David looked interested. 'Is that a euphemism? I met a few ex-MI6 for that TV series I was in. Their families would have said something similar.'

Morgana paused before answering. She could have been pausing for effect, counting in her head, *one morgana blakely, two morgana blakely, three morgana blakely* before responding. Or there might have been something in what David said. 'Darling,' Morgana said eventually, 'I simply have no idea what Piers does. It's worthy but boring. Not the stuff of romantic heroes – or action heroes – I'm afraid.'

'Talking of action heroes,' David said, 'I hear the handyman's missing. I'll go and look for him. Where would he be?'

'Let me think,' said Morgana, 'I've been here often enough... Yes! He's got a shed round the back of the playground where he keeps his tools, next to the landlord's place. You could try there.'

David went off in search of Dizzy.

Morgana said, 'I think I'll go and see if Victoria needs help pacifying the non-prizewinning parents. I'll offer to send off a few signed books, that usually helps. If things get really fractious, I might have to agree to judge an under-sixteens flash fiction writing competition or something. Remember that time, a few years ago, Muriel, when we thought we'd have to get up and sing a song to calm everyone down?'

'I'm not sure it would have had a calming effect,' said Dr. Muriel. 'Everything seems much more under control here today. I doubt we'll feel called upon to participate in the performance.'

'You will come and join me soon, won't you?' said Morgana. 'The show will be starting any minute. Don't let me take my place on that stage all alone. Some of the numbers would seem interminably long if they weren't punctuated by your derisive snorting, cheering things along.'

When Morgana had gone, Dr. Muriel got up and closed the door. She said, 'I had a look at that letter. Curious, don't you think?'

'What does it say?

Dr. Muriel took a note that had been written in blue biro on blue stationery from her pocket and showed it to Emily before putting it back in her pocket again.

THE SHOW MUST GO ON
OR MUST IT NOT?
STOP IT, VICKY
OR BE STOPPED

'It seems to be a threat to disrupt the show, but it doesn't make much sense,' Emily said. 'There's no consistency or clarity about what they want her to do, even if she were inclined to follow their directions. It's as if sending the notes is more important than the threats they contain. The first note seemed to be a threat to tell Piers, then to tell everyone, then to tell people at the school. Maybe the sender just wants to frighten her rather than get her to do anything. It seems to be a bluff, doesn't it? I mean, we've all got secrets.'

'Interesting! And very perceptive. Here's another curious thing: Why would someone send a letter here all of a sudden when they had been sending them to her house?'

'Victoria thinks David sent them.'

'Do you?'

'No. But she thinks it's connected to the video, and no one knew about it except her and David and a few of the other students – and their tutor who watched it, who died.'

'That's what she says. But she really is a most indiscreet person. We'd be hard-pressed to find someone in this building who didn't know about the video. You and I and Morgana know. And Seema and Graham.'

'And Dizzy – and Mr. Barrymore. I think he was listening at the door when she mentioned it. But most of them only heard about it today.'

'Indeed. The question is, who knew *before* those letters started arriving. And why send them in the first place? If it was David, what would he hope to achieve? We need to take a look at that video, Emily.'

'It's gone missing. And so has Dizzy.'

'Well, David is looking for Dizzy, so let's you and I hunt the video together. Where should we look?'

'There's a cupboard somewhere with a video cart with a TV and video player on it. Seema mentioned it. We could try there. I'm not quite sure where it is...'

'Perfect! Can't be hard to find.'

Dr. Muriel opened the door to the office, and they set off. They tried the handles of the doors as they passed. Most opened onto classrooms. One opened onto a staffroom. One opened onto a small kitchen with a fridge, a kettle and a microwave. Eventually they found a door that looked promising. It was marked 'AV Cupboard', and it was locked or blocked from the inside. As Emily and Dr. Muriel pressed their weight against it, they heard the sound of David's mellifluous voice behind them. 'Maybe the door opens outwards, ladies. Have you tried it?'

He reached through their arms and tried it, but the door did not open outwards. It opened inwards like the others, and it was stuck. David laughed. He said, 'Sorry. I didn't mean to be a patronising git.'

'Any luck with finding Dizzy, David?' Dr. Muriel asked him. 'Did you see him?'

'Didn't see anyone except the landlord at the sink at his kitchen window – at least I suppose it was the landlord. Wearing an England shirt? Thuggish-looking bloke. But he gave me a big smile.'

'That sounds like a very practical and comfortable solution to the question of how best to avoid Victoria's end-of-term show,' said Dr. Muriel. 'Warm and cosy in his kitchen, out of sight and sound of a hundred-odd children, no doubt putting the kettle on. No wonder he was smiling.' She turned back to the door. 'Let's try this, then. On my count: one, two, three.'

The three of them pushed, and the door opened a little way and then opened further. It was blocked by a man's body lying on the floor. The man was wearing dark blue overalls. It was Dizzy.

David went over to him and put his fingers on Dizzy's neck to check if he was alive. Dizzy groaned, looked up, and said, 'Great admirer of your work, man.'

'You've been knocked unconscious,' said David. 'Looks like a blow to the back of your head.'

'Have I? Woah! How long have I been out? I was having this really nice dream.'

'Did you bring the video up here, Dizzy?' asked Dr. Muriel.

'I've got aspirations,' said Dizzy, sitting up and touching the back of his head delicately with his fingers. 'Acting – I'm drawn to the profession. That's why I work at this place. David Devereux: household name. Thought if I watched a vid from his early days, I might learn something.'

Emily stepped over him and pressed the narrow letterbox opening on the video player with her fingers. It flapped inwards, gently. She pressed the eject button anyway, just in case, but there was nothing in the machine. 'There's nothing here now,' she said.

'Perhaps we should get you to a hospital,' Dr. Muriel said to Dizzy. She leaned in to him and waggled her hand in his face. 'How many fingers am I holding up?'

'Three. No, two. No, three.'

'Sounds OK to me,' said Dr. Muriel. 'Of course, I'm not a medical doctor.'

'Someone knocked you on the head and stole the video?' asked Emily.

'Could be,' said Dizzy. 'Could be. They might of misunderstood the nature of the content of it. There's some unsavoury people about.'

'You didn't see who it was?' Emily asked.

'I didn't, Emily. Must of been a fella, though. Gave me a pretty good whack.'

Emily turned to David. 'You didn't see anything suspicious?' she asked. *When you were wandering around unaccompanied, supposedly looking for the man we've just found unconscious?*

'What's going on?' It was Victoria's voice behind them. She was now dressed in a smart black trouser suit, ready to host the afternoon's event. Emily was relieved to see that she was not wearing the shawl.

'Don't worry, Victoria,' said Emily. 'He's not dead.'

Victoria said, 'Everyone's downstairs ready to watch the show – everyone except you, Dr. Muriel – and I can't find that wretched dog. Fortunately Graham and I can improvise. I think I have an "invisible dog" lead in the cupboard in the office. Who's not dead?'

'I'm not,' called Dizzy.

Victoria headed for the office, and they all went along with her – perhaps everyone was as curious as Emily to see what an 'invisible dog lead' might be. When they got there, they saw Seema and a police officer. Seema looked as though she had been crying.

'I told him you've got a show to put on,' Seema said to Victoria. 'I asked if he could wait to question you till afterwards, and he said yes.'

'Question me? What on earth about? *Is* someone dead?'

'No!' called Dizzy from the back of the group.

'Yes,' said the police officer. He was quite young, and he looked like a fitness instructor, which was a job he did in his spare time. 'Mr. Barrymore, your landlord. They found him at his place.'

'How long ago did he die?' asked Emily.

'I'm afraid I can't divulge. They're going through all that now. It looks as though he's been dead for some hours.'

'Was he watching a video?' asked Victoria.

'I can't say, madam.'

'Just tell me this.' Victoria's voice was slightly unsteady. She put her hands one on top of the other and placed them just under her clavicle as she drew a deep breath. She said, 'Was he smiling when he died? Would you say he had a rictus grin on his face?'

'I wouldn't say something like that, madam. That's not the sort of terminology we use in the reports.'

'Was anyone with him?' asked Emily.

'Only a dog. A bulldog. I'm afraid the animal is also deceased.'

'Who would kill a dog?' asked Emily. Now she was upset.

The policeman looked sympathetic. He turned towards Emily and put his hand out as though he was considering touching her arm to comfort her. But he didn't approach her. 'The dog wasn't killed, miss. It looked like natural causes.'

'Of course it did,' said Victoria. 'Of course it did.' She shook her head back and forth several times.

Seema said, 'The show's about to start. What do you want to do, Victoria? You want to call it off?'

'I'll go down,' said Victoria, 'and we'll carry on as if nothing had happened. If the children only learn from me that we have to carry on *no matter what happens in our personal lives*, they'll have learned the most important lesson about this profession... Officer, it's very kind of you to be so understanding. I'll talk to you when the show's over. Say about half past five? Dizzy? If you're well enough, I'll need you to operate the sound and lights, please.'

Victoria left the office, followed by Dizzy.

The policeman said, 'Does that lady think this is a murder enquiry?'

Seema said, 'I didn't do anything. I'm not responsible for what happened.' She looked as though she might cry again. She also left the office.

David said, 'I'd better go and find Dolly.' He took his mobile phone out of his pocket and looked at it, then put it back again. 'I'll keep this on silent.'

Emily, Dr. Muriel and the policeman were left in the office. The policeman said, 'Didn't I see you two at that bonfire party in the big house down the end of Trinity Road?'

'Wasn't that fun!' said Dr. Muriel, standing and making shovelling motions with her hands so he would see himself out.

Just before he closed the door to the office, the policeman said, 'The video that might hypothetically be in the video player of the house of the gentleman who died. What sort of video was it, do you think?'

'It was a video Victoria made when she was a student at drama school,' said Emily.

'Ah!' he said. 'I see.'

'Not that kind of video,' Emily said, closing the door.

When he had gone, she asked Dr. Muriel, 'If you really liked someone but you thought they might have done something stupid, should you speak up about it even though they might get in trouble?'

'Aha!' said Dr. Muriel. 'Now, we'll be addressing all sorts of questions like this at the next conference in Eastbourne. Or is it Torquay? Anyhow, it would be wonderful to have you come along and listen to some of the finest minds in Europe debate such conundrums, both trivial and meaningful. It gets very heated. Most amusing. There is no right or wrong, of course. Only brilliant arguments from all sides.'

'What I'm trying to say,' said Emily, 'is do you think David could have bashed Dizzy on the head? He was gone for ages before he suddenly "found" him with us.'

'He doesn't strike me as a basher. And what's his motivation? No, it doesn't follow.'

'But then he said he waved and smiled at Mr. Barrymore in his kitchen window. But the policeman said that Mr. Barrymore had been dead for some time.'

'Indeed, indeed – most suspicious. But, although that young policeman wasn't prepared to say anything, I do think Mr. Barrymore might have been watching Vicky's video, don't you?'

'Yes.'

'So it follows that if Mr. Barrymore stole that video, then it was probably Mr. B who bashed Dizzy.'

'Yes. But you don't think the *video* killed Mr. Barrymore, surely?'

'No, I don't... Good Lord!'

'What?'

'What's that frightful noise?'

Emily had also heard the noise coming from downstairs. It was a sawing sound. Last-minute repairs? Perhaps Dizzy's head injury had been more serious than anyone realised and he was running amok with power tools. She listened carefully. 'I think it might be the Flight of the Bumblebee.'

'Good. Good. First song of the afternoon. It means we've got a long, long time till the prize-giving. Morgana will never forgive me if I don't sit through the show and watch it with her, but I've put up with worse things than Morgana's unforgiveness. Come on. We need to do a little sleuthing for ourselves. We know what we do not have: we do not have a video that is such bad luck or so horrendous to watch that it kills people, because that would be daft. We do not have an actor who is a murderer. We do have an injured man, a dead man and a dead dog.'

'And we have poison pen letters,' said Emily. 'I have a theory about who might have sent those.'

'Do you? Marvellous! Then we'll do some confronting later on.'

'Not on stage? Not in front of the children?'

'No, my dear. That would be a denouncement. That wouldn't do at all. A denouncement is public and upsetting. A confrontation is by invitation only and most satisfying. We'll do the confronting shortly before the policeman comes back, perhaps. When all the parents and the children are gone.'

'What if that policeman wasn't a real policeman? What if he was an actor who'd been hired to pretend that Mr. Barrymore was dead, to frighten Victoria?'

'He was rather young and handsome, wasn't he? He recognised us, though, didn't he? And he seemed rather sweet on you. He kept smiling and looking at your arm. No, I'm afraid there's nothing else for it. We have to go and confront the thing we fear most.'

'Victoria's video?'

'Only indirectly. No, I meant death.'

Emily and Dr. Muriel went back down the stairs, meaning to reach Mr. Barrymore's home by cutting across the playground. Before they got to the door that led outside, they passed the assembly hall and peeked in through a small window set into the door at about head height. Around two dozen small children were on stage, dressed in black and yellow striped costumes. Dizzy was at the technician's desk, operating the spotlights, sound effects and backing tapes.

The parents and siblings of the students were a warm and appreciative audience. At the front, positioned to half-face the stage, half-face the audience – like the Queen at a command performance of the Royal Variety Show – Morgana sat alone between an empty chair that had been meant for Midori, the Japanese DJ with the delicate constitution who had cancelled due to illness, and an empty chair that was meant for Dr. Muriel, the hearty British professor who would rather face death than sit through a musical theatre show by Victoria's students.

They started to creep away from the assembly hall towards the door to the playground but hadn't gone more than two or three steps before Victoria came up behind them and stopped them. She was back in her blue pinafore, though this time she was wearing red Wellington boots rather than sparkly shoes. 'Funnier, don't you think? And anyway I'm not going to do the tap routine. Graham's an incompetent hoofer, though I can hardly blame him. It's my fault for leaving it so late to rehearse.'

Victoria's hair was braided into two plaits again. She had an 'invisible dog' lead in her right hand – a stiff piece of red leather that reached almost to her ankles when she held the top loop of it at waist height, with a circle of red leather at the bottom, facing forward, as though strained by the neck of a smallish, eager dog that Emily and Dr. Muriel could not see.

'I'm going to go to the police after the show and confess everything,' Victoria said. 'That video has done enough damage. I've got blood on my hands. Piers will be relieved, at least. He thinks I spend too much time at Showstoppers and not enough time at home.'

'Where is Piers?' asked Dr. Muriel. 'I'd have thought he'd be here to support you.'

'I know,' said Victoria with cool irony. 'What sort of man puts Queen and country before his wife's end-of-term show at her drama school?'

'The sort of man who doesn't want his wife to have a nervous breakdown,' said Dr. Muriel.

Victoria put her right hand to her eyebrows and leaned forward and swivelled a half turn on her right heel as though she planned to dance the hornpipe. But she was only manoeuvring to look through the window in the door to the assembly hall. 'Ugh,' she said. 'Did you notice that? The lights keep dipping, and there's something not right with the sound levels. If Mr. Barrymore weren't dead, I'd kill him myself.'

'I suppose you won't have to move the school now that he's dead?' said Emily.

Victoria twisted her mouth, as if she was slightly ashamed of herself for what she had just said. 'Yes. I hadn't thought about that... Poor old Barry. The electrics are playing up, and he's not even here, so I feel a bit guilty that I ever implied he could be responsible. Though I do have my suspicions that the infant toilets won't be blocking up again in future... Where *are* you two going? Don't let the kids see you if you're nipping outside for a smoke. And please, please, please make sure you come back for at least part of the show. The finale's going to be great. I've had a brainwave and changed *everything* at the last minute.'

'We won't miss your teachers' skit,' said Dr. Muriel. 'What a shame you won't be tap dancing. That's always my favourite part.'

'Don't you worry, we're all coming on at the end – teachers, tinies, teenagers – and we're doing a group tap dance then. Samuel has briefed them, and they adore him and listen to what he says, so I hope it won't be too chaotic. Graham and I will just be singing for our skit, and I'll do a bit of business with the dog lead, and maybe a cartwheel, and hope these boots don't fall off. Graham has a wonderful voice, but the less he moves on stage this afternoon, the better, or we won't have anyone sign up for dance class and choreography next term and Seema will have my guts for garters.'

'Where is Seema?' asked Emily.

'She's taken the screwdriver, and she's gone to have a look at the fuse box under the stage, even though I've begged her to leave it alone. She's very tight-fisted with the accounts, so maybe she feels responsible for being a cheapskate and not getting a qualified electrician in, and she's trying to make amends. Although, doing it by killing herself is not the best way. Don't you think?'

'Well, if we see her, we'll intervene,' said Dr. Muriel. 'We don't want another dead body or a serious injury.'

'Oh, I don't think there's any question of that now that the video is at Barry's house under police guard. I do feel a tremendous amount of relief, actually. So long as it's evidence, they'll have to keep it under lock and key. And after that I'll just ask them to destroy it for me. I'm sure they'll be glad to help as I'm going to cooperate fully – it should keep the paperwork down.'

'You're not seriously going to confess to murder?' asked Emily.

'Living in a house with one man and three teenage boys, I sometimes think that going to prison is the only way I could get any peace,' said Victoria. 'But no, I'm not going to confess to killing anyone. Piers is right. Dr. Muriel's right. A video can't really be bad luck, no matter that David and I used to joke about it after our poor tutor died. But ever since that video turned up at the house, there's been trouble. I wonder if someone's heard me talk about the history of it and they're trying to frame me – I can't think *who* because I hardly breathed a word to anybody.'

'Indeed,' said Dr. Muriel. 'Interesting theory. Here's another for you: might someone be trying to attach some scandal to the name of David Devereux?'

'Could be.'

'Do you still think David sent you those letters?' asked Emily.

'I rather liked Morgana's theory that perhaps he was sending them because he wanted to get my attention, maybe even as a way of getting back together with me. But earlier on today, when I held his hand for the first time after all those years, there was no spark. And Dolly's no pathetic invention to give him an excuse to visit the school – she really is his daughter. She looks just like him.'

'Still, someone sent the letters,' said Emily.

'And whoever it was threatened to stop the show in the latest note,' said Dr. Muriel.

'Did they, indeed? I shan't say "over my dead body!"' said Victoria with a wink. The music coming from the assembly hall changed to jolly, comedic piano music, played very fast. 'Oof!' Victoria said. 'Good old Samuel! That number's the one before mine and Graham's – I'd better go.' She adjusted the invisible dog lead, pretending the unseen animal was tugging at the collar. With a backward flick of her head and a jaunty kick of her right foot, she dashed off after it in time to the music, towards the classroom nearest the assembly hall that was serving as a dressing room for the show.

Emily and Dr. Muriel went into the playground. The hopscotch-covered tarmac of the primary school days was now converted into a pleasant courtyard seating area, with wooden benches and raised flower-beds, and shady areas provided by wooden arches covered in vines and clematis, the landscaping reminiscent of holidays Victoria and Piers had enjoyed in Provence.

They could see the shed at the far end of it, where Dizzy kept his tools. Next to it, within the walled perimeter of the grounds, abutting the school building, was the caretaker's cottage that had been the home of the landlord, Mr. Barrymore. A thin blue and white strip of police tape ran between the front of the cottage and the playground.

Dr. Muriel put her hands in her pockets and strolled next to Emily in a hopelessly suspicious-looking way, as though she were a prisoner of war in a German camp, planning to distribute sand dug from an escape tunnel onto the ground as they walked. Emily was worried that at any minute her companion might actually start whistling.

'I've got a bad feeling about all this,' Emily said. 'The poison pen letters were meant to frighten

Victoria, but now that the video's no longer in her possession, the notes no longer have any effect. I think Victoria might be in danger.'

'Do you know, m'dear, I agree with you.'

'Should we go and stand guard by the stage, in case we need to do something? Or should we call the police?'

'Knowledge is what we need: "intel". If we don't know what we're looking for, we won't know how to stop it. I don't suppose we can get inside the house here, but there's nothing to stop us peering through the window. First things first: the shed.'

The door to the shed was padlocked and didn't open when they pulled at it. They stood side by side at the two small square windows on it and looked into the darkness inside. But nothing looked out of place or suspicious. They turned and stood with their backs to the shed and looked over to Mr. Barrymore's home, to their right. It was also in darkness. The kitchen window faced them. It appeared to be positioned above a sink, where Mr. Barrymore might very well have stood and smiled at David Devereux while he was doing the dishes or filling the kettle for a cup of tea – if only he hadn't already been dead.

'The policeman didn't say where they found him,' said Emily. 'If someone wanted to frame Victoria for murder, or make David look like a liar, could they have propped Mr. Barrymore's body up there, at the sink?'

'Interesting,' said Dr. Muriel. 'It makes a liar of David, certainly. But it doesn't put Victoria at the scene.'

Dr. Muriel pressed the end of her stick into the blue and white tape, moving it close enough to the cottage so that she and Emily could press their faces up against the glass of the living room window. They could see the young policeman inside in the gloom. 'You know,' said Emily, 'if someone wanted to harm Victoria or at least humiliate her and stop the show, wouldn't they choose her *Wizard of Oz* number to do it?'

'We're running out of time, then, m'dear. We urgently need to get ourselves a clue.'

The policeman came to the door of the house and opened it. He looked at Emily, and his hand floated up towards her elbow, tenderly. He didn't quite touch her, and he let his hand drop again as he said, 'Don't worry about the dog, miss. I don't think it suffered at all.'

Emily said, 'You can call me Emily.'

'James,' said the policeman.

'Constable James,' said Dr. Muriel, 'what are you doing lurking about in the gloom back there? Even at your young age, it can't be very good for your sight.'

'The fuse has gone. All the electricity's off.'

'Has it, has it, has it, is it?' said Dr. Muriel. 'Hmmmm. Dodgy wiring, perhaps? Tell me, was he found here in the kitchen, holding on to the taps?'

'You know I can't tell you that, madam.'

'Doctor.'

'Do you need one?' The policeman looked alarmed. His hand floated up, now, towards Dr. Muriel's elbow.'

'You may call me "doctor". But I don't insist on it. As you wish.'

'Oh, I see.' James looked at Emily and widened his eyes a bit to signal that he hoped she'd let on whether or not Dr. Muriel was teasing him. Emily grinned back.

'Were the taps metal?' said Dr. Muriel. 'Can you tell me that?'

'Well, I don't see what else they'd be made of,' said the policeman, a bit sulkily.

Dr. Muriel said, 'Here are the facts, as you have hinted at them or (in the case of the taps) confirmed them: Mr. Barrymore, a most unscrupulous landlord, a saver of pennies and cutter of corners, was found here at the sink, gripping the metal taps and staring out the window, with a ghastly grin on his face. The electricity was off, a fuse apparently having blown.' Dr. Muriel turned to Emily. 'What do you make of that, Emily?'

'The metal taps were live, somehow? He went to fill the kettle or wash his hands and he was electrocuted, and that caused a short circuit and blew a fuse?'

'Precisely!'

'Well, yes,' conceded James the policeman. 'It could be something like that.'

'The bulldog, Precious, was lying in the living room, teeth bared in the approximation of a human smile, having been electrocuted also because some part of her body was touching a lamp or some other electrical apparatus, which had also gone live.'

'She didn't suffer at all,' James said to Emily. 'I really think she didn't.'

'That's very clever,' said Emily to Dr. Muriel. 'Shouldn't you save it all for the confrontation?'

'That wasn't the confrontation, it was the denouement. And yes, I'll have to go through it all again. But let's consider it a dress rehearsal. It is a show business event, after all.'

'So it was natural causes?' Emily said. 'That means Victoria's not in danger. David Devereux's not a liar. We can go in and watch the show.'

'David Devereux?' said James. 'The actor in that spy thing? Isn't he supposed to be going to Hollywood?'

'Goodbye, Constable,' said Dr. Muriel. 'Come, Emily. If we hurry, we'll catch Victoria's performance. She's a talented actor, with wonderful comic timing. I won't say she's wasted here, but there's no match for her in any of the shows currently playing in the West End.'

They rushed back to the assembly hall, where they waited for the sound of applause to signal the end of the current number before Emily slipped in discreetly at the back of the audience, while Dr. Muriel went through a side door and took her place next to Morgana Blakely, whose face was so pinched with fury at being left alone that it looked as though her features were trying to shrink themselves to match the size of the tiny top hat she was wearing.

There was a space in a row at the back, three seats in next to David Devereux – the only space Emily could see, though she didn't look very hard. David saw her approaching, bent low as though she was a giantess who feared catching her hair in overhead pylons, and he moved up and moved Dolly up next to him, so Emily could take the seat on the end. He smiled and put his arm across the back of Dolly and reached to Emily's shoulder and gave it a squeeze, pressing his leg into Dolly's and Dolly's whole body into Emily, so for a moment they were all three of them scrunched up and cute-looking like a family of foxes in a den.

'Victoria'll be hilarious!' he whispered. 'If she's anything like she was at drama school. Wait till you see this.'

To the right, about halfway down the auditorium, Emily noticed a gleam of white as Seema edged her way in and stood quietly watching, back against the wall. White trousers really were distracting when worn by audience members, Emily thought. It was almost as bad as people eating popcorn in the cinema or texting on their mobile phones. Because of the trousers, she couldn't help tracking Seema's movements as she moved slowly to the back of the hall and then went to stand by Dizzy, where he operated the mixing desk for the sound and lights for the show.

Emily wasn't a regular theatre-goer, and she found she was summarising her reactions to the performance as though sending postcards to herself: *Victoria was very funny, and Graham was a little stiff in his movements but had an extraordinarily deep and attractive vibrato voice. Victoria's cartwheel was hilarious! 'Somewhere Over the Rainbow' was beautiful, and when she sang it, a capella, Victoria made almost everyone cry.*

Dolly held Emily's left hand in her right hand, and her father's right hand in her left as she sat between them. Emily wished that everyone she had ever known – everyone she had ever worked for or with in a temp contract in a miserable job – could be here to see their little group and speculate that Emily was somehow connected to David Devereux.

She sent herself a little postcard about it: *On her way to Hollywood!*

David leaned over and whispered, 'She's great, isn't she? Remind me to tell you about this video we made when we were students. It was hilarious. You'll laugh your socks off.'

Remind me to tell you *when*? When we're on a date? When you come to pick me up from my next temp job in your Bentley or your Lamborghini? When we're flying to Hollywood together?

David bent and kissed Dolly's adorable head. He laughed as if Victoria's *Wizard of Oz* skit was the funniest thing he had ever seen and this was the happiest day of his life. His laughter carried, and a few people looked round to see what was going on and then smiled when they saw it was David Devereux, and he really was laughing at the show. Behind them, Emily was aware that Seema was agitated, whispering to Dizzy about something. Perhaps she was disappointed that there was to be no tap dancing routine from Victoria? Or perhaps she was jealous that Emily was sitting next to the world's most good-natured handsome man.

In the classroom across the corridor that was serving as a dressing room, out of sight of the audience, all the members of Showstoppers were assembled, their small sweaty feet laced into their tap shoes, ready to take the stage for the final number, their small sweaty hands linked together as they prepared to come on in tightly-squished, snaking rows and then form one big circle together.

Victoria and Graham took their bow. Next to Emily, David whooped and blew three wolf whistles through his fingers. Victoria smiled and nodded her head once in his direction in acknowledgement, one professional to another, just like any other seasoned performer glad to see that one of their kind is 'in' to see the show.

'Brava!' shouted Dr. Muriel in her seat near the front, for all the world as if she were at the opera in Italy, where it's usual to match the gender of the exclamation to the person who is being praised. 'Brava!' If she had meant the praise for both Graham and Victoria, she would have shouted 'Bravi! Had her praise been meant just for Graham, she would have shouted 'Bravo!' Presumably she meant no offence to Graham by singling out Victoria – they were neighbours, after all. And

Victoria was the school's artistic director and owner. Also, her cartwheel had been magnificent, as had her 'Somewhere Over the Rainbow'.

Victoria and Graham left the stage with a final wave to the audience, Victoria pretending to be led off by the invisible dog, to the amusement of Dolly and the other children in the audience, who shrieked in recognition of a kind of magic that needed them to 'see' it and believe in its charming illusion. Emily thought of her dog, Jessie, who had died and left a kind of invisible dog in her place which Emily 'saw' sometimes when she was tired or lonely, or when she simply forgot that Jessie had died. She wasn't too old to believe in magic, even if it made her feel sad sometimes.

The lights went down, and there was no music, only the swelling sound, stage left – to the right of the audience – of a hundred pairs of tap shoes beginning to beat a rhythm in the dressing room as the children prepared to come on. *It was very theatrical! So effective!* Emily postcarded to herself, enjoying the build-up. She began to think she should go to the theatre more often.

The children began to cross the corridor from the dressing room, heading towards the back of the stage where they would come on, though their performance had already begun. The sound of their tapping feet grew louder.

'Oh my God!' shrieked Seema white trousers gleaming where she now stood where she had first come in at the side of auditorium. 'Oh my God! Tap shoes! They're wearing tap shoes! All them sweaty little feet in metal and leather! Oh my God! Oh my God!'

Emily thought that if she were in charge of this place – which she was not because if the past was anything to go by, then for the rest of her life she was only ever going to have crappy administrative jobs, working for others, for a pitiful wage – she would send Seema on a management course to help her cope with change. Victoria had decided at the last minute to put the children in tap shoes for the final number. So what? So far, it sounded great.

But Dr. Muriel was on her feet at the front now, waving her walking stick in the air. 'Emily!' she shouted. Dr. Muriel was not the sort to try to storm the stage at a children's end-of-term show so she could join in the dancing – she had plenty of limelight during her day job, where she frequently addressed large conferences on her specialist subjects: ethics and philosophical conundrums. Even if Dr. Muriel did plan to storm the stage, there was no reason for her to call for Emily to join in. So it was something else...

Suddenly, Emily understood.

She jumped to her feet. She rushed to the technician's desk where Dizzy was standing and began pulling at wires and plugs, screaming, 'Turn it off! Turn it off!' If she could just expose two live wires and touch them together, she might stand a chance of tripping the fuse and killing the power – if she didn't kill herself first.

At the front, Dr. Muriel had whisked Morgana Blakely's miniature top hat from her head and now skimmed it onto the stage, where it skidded across the boards, sparking as the mesh veil attached to the hat and the hat pins that had secured it caught on a live wire or wires poking from beneath the stage, not far from the spot where Victoria had been performing her *Wizard of Oz* routine.

Morgana got to her feet and took action. 'No children on stage!' she commanded. 'Victoria, do you hear me? Graham! Don't let the children on the stage!'

Graham the Tin Man appeared through the side door in the assembly hall nearest to the stage, trying to make sense of what was going on. Dr. Muriel didn't hesitate. She grabbed his triangular hat and threw it towards the location of the exposed live wires on stage in front of her. She was a frequent guest lecturer on cruise ships and was an expert player of deck quoits (donut-shaped, heavyish objects made of rubber or rope, guaranteed not to bounce and go over the side), so her missile struck its target effectively. Sparks flew, and a hissing sound came from the stage.

In the background, the ominous thrumming of two hundred tap shoes continued, the children held at bay as Morgana had instructed, though it seemed Victoria was determined that, somehow or other, even if out of sight of the audience, the show would go on.

Dr. Muriel next threw her stick with its metal band around the tip (which didn't have any effect, though it made an impressive rattling sound), then she removed her jacket and threw it metal-button side down, causing more sparks and then, at last –

whether through Dr. Muriel's interventions or Emily's – the fuses blew, the lights went off. Everyone was safe.

There was silence. Even the tap shoes had ceased tapping. There was darkness except for smears of late-afternoon sunlight coming through the cracks in the blackout curtains that had been hung at the tall windows along the left-hand side of the auditorium. Then there was spontaneous, rapturous applause from children and parents, and whoops and whistles, and then the sound of scraping chairs as the audience got to their feet in a standing ovation. At the periphery of her vision, Emily caught a flash of white as Seema turned and ran out through the door at the back of the assembly hall.

Dizzy had seen it, too. 'Oh no you don't, missy!' he called as he rushed out after her.

David Devereux had joined Emily near the technician's desk, where she stood with wires and plugs in her hands. He had Dolly with him – she didn't look frightened. She was young enough to think the finale might have been part of the show.

'Emily!' said David. 'Girl, that was brave of you.'

'*Now* we can have the denouement,' said Emily, shaking a bit – with shock, she thought, rather than electrical energy.

David reached over and grabbed her arm and pulled her towards him, and he kissed her.

So that's what you do when something I say isn't particularly funny, thought Emily. She resolved to be less amusing in front of handsome actors in future.

David's phone rang, and he answered it, 'Yes, yes... Yes! Yeah, I can. Yeah. OK, buddy,' while nodding and pretending to listen to Dolly, who was asking him a question.

'Daddy,' she said, 'is this my new school?'

'No, babe.' He finished his call. He put his hand on Dolly's head, smoothing her gorgeous curls, and he smiled at Emily.

'But I like it here, Daddy. I like Toto. I liked the ninja part at the end.'

David laughed his beautiful laugh, as if inviting the angels to join in. He said, 'Yeah, babe. It's great, isn't it? But I just got the call. We're moving to LA.'

***

A little later on, in Victoria's kitchen at her house opposite the flat where Emily lived, Dr. Muriel – jacket back on, stick propped against the desk – poured tea for Victoria, Emily and a hatless Morgana while they discussed the day's events. It was five o'clock, and they were all rather hungry, so Victoria split and toasted eight spicy fruit tea cakes, two at a time, in her expensive stainless steel toaster, and Emily stood next to her and buttered them and piled them onto a plate. Victoria was back in her jeans, white T-Shirt and pewter shawl, something like her fifth costume change of the day.

It had already been agreed that they had all been wonderful, and very brave, and they had praised each other accordingly. Now they were pondering the motives of the person who had nearly killed a hundred children on a Saturday afternoon in south London.

'Seema sent those poison pen letters?' asked Morgana.

'It was a bit of a giveaway when she produced another one this morning, saying it had been sent to Showstoppers instead of being sent to your house,' said Emily, taking her place at the table and picking up her cup of tea.

'As if I didn't have enough to worry about,' said Victoria, 'with the end-of-term show.'

'That was rather the point,' said Dr. Muriel. 'Seema thought the letters would tip you over the edge and you would stand down from running the school and let her take your place. She was very jealous of your success.'

'And like a lot of people who aren't very bright,' said Emily, 'she couldn't see why you were in charge and she wasn't. She liked following processes, and she found your creative management style irritating and threatening, especially your last-minute changes of plan. She thought that all she had to do was replace you, instead of learning the skills that would earn her the right to take over.'

'But I don't get it,' said Victoria, bringing the plate of tea cakes to the table and taking a seat next to Morgana. 'How did she know about the video?'

'You told her,' said Dr. Muriel, stretching for a tea cake. 'You told everyone.'

'Yes, but not until today.' Victoria nudged the plate in Dr. Muriel's direction so she could reach the food without embarrassing herself.

'You told me yesterday,' Emily said.

'You must have told Seema about the video a while ago,' said Dr. Muriel. 'I'd guess it was not long after your tutor's widow sent it to you out of the blue.'

'Poor Bill,' said Victoria, chomping on a buttery toasted tea cake. 'I don't remember saying anything to Seema. But she was a very good listener – she always seemed so sympathetic.'

'You didn't feel you could say anything to Piers,' said Morgana. 'Who else were you to turn to?'

'And you are terribly indiscreet,' said Dr. Muriel, offering the plate of tea cakes to Emily. 'I knew that Emily had lost her job, for example, only hours after Emily herself had told you.'

'Oh, Ems,' said Victoria. 'I know I offered you some work, but I think you might need to go back to the agency on Monday. I'm not sure we'll be up and running at Showstoppers for a while. You know?'

'That's OK, Victoria,' said Emily. 'I'm used to it. Thanks for asking me, anyway. You did tell Seema about that video. Then when David tried to enrol Dolly at Showstoppers, it gave Seema the idea of sending the poison pen letters and hinting that David was responsible, to upset you.'

'But what about Mr. Barrymore?' said Victoria. 'Yes, he was an ugly, bald fat man in an England shirt who tried to get me to give up my school premises so he could turn it into overpriced flats for young professionals – but that didn't mean he deserved to die.'

'He was the one who knocked Dizzy on the head,' said Emily. 'He'd been standing at the door to the office and overheard that there was a video you'd made with your boyfriend when you were a drama student. I think maybe he thought it would be, you know...'

'Stimulating, rather than artistic,' said Dr. Muriel, dabbing with a handkerchief at a spot of melted butter that had dripped onto her jersey.

'He certainly seemed very keen to get a look at it,' said Emily. 'I can't believe I thought David might have bashed Dizzy.'

'It's not such an outrageous idea,' said Dr. Muriel. 'After all, David Devereux does sometimes seem to be too good to be true.'

'Never mind him,' said Morgana. 'Wasn't there also a dog that died? Killing a dog is unforgiveable.'

'I think Seema was responsible for the death of both landlord and dog,' said Dr. Muriel. 'The police are interviewing her now, of course. But I think they'll discover her motive was to drive Victoria to have a nervous breakdown and hand over the daily running of the school to Seema, while also removing any worries about Showstoppers having to move to new premises, of course. It wasn't very far from the school to the landlord's cottage. Seema could have nipped down there at any time and tampered with the wiring – she seemed to fancy herself as something of dab hand electrician, on top of everything else.'

Emily continued, 'The "rictus smile" on Barrymore's and Precious's faces was caused by the electric shocks they received when Seema went to the cottage and tampered with the wiring earlier this morning. Seema would have seen Dizzy swipe the video from her desk and then seen Mr Barrymore sneaking off after him–'

Dr. Muriel interrupted excitedly, 'And she'd have known she had just enough time to go to the cottage and wire up the taps in the kitchen. The current passing through him would have made the landlord's body stiffen, his hands gripping the taps and keeping him standing upright. It would have contorted his face into something that David Devereux might have mistaken for a smile as he walked past the kitchen window.'

'Mr. Barrymore didn't die laughing,' said Emily, 'though when you asked James, the police constable, and he didn't deny it, Victoria, it fitted with your "dying of laughter" theory about the video. Of course, Seema knew it would.'

Dr. Muriel said to Victoria, 'But still you refused to give up on the show and stand down from the school. So next Seema tried tinkering with the wiring at the school so that when the metal of your tap shoe struck the live wires poking out from just under the stage, you'd get a shock. The faulty wiring would be blamed on Mr. Barrymore or Dizzy, or both.'

'Poor Dizzy!' said Morgana.

'Poor old Barrymore!' said Dr. Muriel.

'Poor Precious,' said Emily.

'I feel very ashamed that I didn't realise Dizzy had acting aspirations,' said Victoria. 'You know he's the one who chased down Seema and held onto her until the police arrived? He'd do anything for this place – he doesn't always do it very well, of course. But he does it with a true heart and a great deal of enthusiasm. I've put in a good word at our old drama school. He's auditioning for a summer school for mature students. David Devereux is going to coach him for his audition speech before he gets on the plane to Hollywood.'

'Why did David try to enrol his daughter at Showstoppers if he knew he might be going to LA?' asked Emily.

Victoria laughed, slightly bitterly. 'If every actor who had ever got the call from Hollywood – or been told they were down to the last two for a part in a movie or a starring role in the theatre – if every one of those actors just put their life on hold and waited to hear if it would happen, then they'd never get married; their children would never get an education; their bills would never get paid. You have to assume it will never happen and go about your business accordingly and get your car taxed and pay your TV licence and enrol your children for music lessons and stage school and state school. If it happens, as least you can cancel. If it doesn't, well... at least you're covered for the basics, and you can work towards the next audition and hope it will happen for you next time.'

'Victoria's still up for Desdemona in Branagh's *Othello*,' said Morgana.

'Technically,' said Victoria. 'Though that was nearly twenty years ago, and the film has been made and shown in cinemas and is now available on DVD. I think if they cast me in that part now I'd be inclined to sit up in bed and punch his lights out if Othello tried to stifle me.'

'Punch whose lights out?' asked Emily, impressed. 'Othello's or Kenneth Branagh's?'

'Emily and I have tried to piece together Seema's movements,' said Dr. Muriel, making an effort to get the conversation back to the events of that afternoon. 'The memory of a glimpse of her white trousers every now and then has worked like a very low-tech tracking device.' She chortled at the idea of it. 'She disappeared just before your *Wizard of Oz* number – we think she was under the stage with a screwdriver – and reappeared again to watch the results of her handiwork.'

'I wonder if Seema thought it would kill me,' said Victoria. 'Or if she just wanted to give me a shock.'

They heard the sound of the key in the lock, then Piers' voice calling out as he came through the door after a day at work. 'Victoria?'

They heard Piers hang up his coat, find a place for his laptop computer, wash his hands in the sink in the downstairs bathroom.

Morgana said to Victoria, 'With your last-minute change of plan, all those children in tap shoes with metal plates on the bottom for the finale, in a big snaky line, joined together with damp hands and sweaty feet...' She shuddered. 'What might have happened just doesn't bear thinking about.'

Victoria called out to her husband, 'In here, darling!'

'Thank God you're home,' he said as he walked into the kitchen. 'You won't believe the day I've had.'

By the same author:

ALISON WONDERLAND
Only occasionally does a piece of fiction leap out and demand immediate cult status. Alison Wonderland is one.
The Times

Smith is gin-and-tonic funny.
Booklist

BEING LIGHT
Smith has a keen eye for material details, but her prose is lucid and uncluttered by heavy description. Imagine a satire on Cool Britannia made by the Coen Brothers.
Times Literary Supplement

This is a novel in which the ordinary and the unusual are constantly juxtaposed in various idiosyncratic characters... Its airy quirkiness is a delight.
The Times

A screwball comedy that really works.
The Independent

By the same author:

THE MIRACLE INSPECTOR
The Miracle Inspector is one of the few novels that
everyone should read, it's a powerful novel that's
masterfully written and subtly complex.
SciFi and Fantasy Books

Helen Smith crafts a story like she's the British
lovechild of Kurt Vonnegut and Philip K. Dick.
Journal of Always Reviews

About the author:

Helen Smith is a novelist and
playwright who lives in London.
She is the author of Alison
Wonderland, Being Light and
The Miracle Inspector as well as
the Emily Castles mysteries.

39198292R10065

Made in the USA
San Bernardino, CA
21 September 2016